For my children Courtney and Zahra (thanks for the inspiration) and my nieces Stephanie and Sarah. My eternal gratitude and love to my partner Graham, for believing in me, and to my mom and dad, who told me the first stories.
L.S.

I dedicate this work to my wonderful wife Christine and my delightful daughters Naomi and Imogen.
M.G.

Published in 2005 by
Simply Read Books in
the US and Canada
www.simplyreadbooks.com

Text copyright @ 2005 Louise Schofield
Illustrations copyright @ 2005 Malcolm Geste

First published by Freemantle Arts Centre Press

Cataloging in Publication Data

Schofield, Louise, 1961 – The Zoo Room / Louise Schofield; illustrated by Malcolm Geste.
ISBN 1-894965-19-1

1. Picture books for children. I. Geste, Malcolm II. Title.
PZ7.S363Zo 2005   j823'.92   C2005-900578-5

Consultant Editor Ray Coffey
Designers Marion Duke and Jody de Haas

10 9 8 7 6 5 4 3 2 1

Printed and bound in Hong Kong

The ZOO ROOM

SIMPLY READ BOOKS

Max and Kelly had an aunt who worked at the zoo. No one saw much of Aunt Zelda because she preferred being with the animals.

But when she came to visit, strange and wonderful things would happen.

Just before Max's birthday, a card arrived by special post. Inside was an invitation to the Zoo Room restaurant. "The Zoo Room?" said Mom. "I've never heard of it."

Max and Kelly could hardly wait for Saturday night! But when they arrived at the zoo, it was closed.

"Shhh! Listen!" said Mom. Strange music drifted over from the other side.

Dad tried the gate. It creaked and squeaked open.

Inside, the animal noises were louder and scarier than they were by day. Monster shadows stretched across the pathway.

Mom pulled a flashlight from her bag. "Follow me," she said. Screeching bats flapped away into the moonlight.

They soon came to a clearing and couldn't believe what they saw. "Hello, Cocky" said a cockatoo as she took Dad's hat and hung it on a branch.

A spider monkey climbed onto Max's shoulder.
"That sister of mine is full of surprises," said Mom. They all agreed anything was possible with Aunt Zelda.

The Zoo Cafe had been transformed into the most amazing restaurant, crowded with animals.

"There seems to be some kind of order to this chaos," said

Dad, checking the tablecloths. "But I think the kangaroos are in the wrong place, don't you?"

"I wonder where we'll be sitting?" said Max.

The red tables were on the scary side with the killer teeth and murderous claws, evil beaks and gnashing jaws.

"Carnivores," said Kelly. "I hope we're not sitting there!"

"That lovely bird had better watch out," said Mom.

On the other side, the herbivores were in a frenzy. A giant gorilla beat his chest.

"That gorilla reminds me of your dad when we first met," laughed Mom. "Now, where is Zelda? Can anyone see her?"

Suddenly, the waiter arrived – all hairy and scary with white pointy teeth. Dad thought his smile was friendly, so . . .

. . . they followed him to their table. The omnivores sat at tables with red and green checks.

"Looks like Zelda's sort of crowd here tonight," said Dad. "I wonder if she'll join us?"

"That frog is sitting at the wrong table," said Kelly.

The waiter smiled (well, they hoped it was a smile) and handed out green and red menus. The choices on the red menu included something interesting called "Beast of the Day". Max wondered if that was what the big cats were eating. . . .

Dad said he'd pass on the snakes, but the chops sounded good.
Kelly wanted sausages.

"And I'll have the fish," said Mom.

Max wanted something a bit different. "Are the insects crunchy?"
he asked. The waiter nodded. "Unreal!" he giggled. "That's what
I'll have."

They sat and watched the other customers while they waited for their orders. Some of the diners were making real pigs of themselves. The kookaburras laughed at a joke.

At last their meals arrived. Max and Kelly were so hungry they forgot their manners, but eating like animals was not a problem at the Zoo Room.

Soon all the plates were empty except for one. Max wouldn't touch his insects. NO WAY!

"You ordered it. You eat it," said Mom firmly.

A prowling tiger appeared and growled.

Max did as he was told.
"Yum, yum, barbecued insects are crunchy and munchy!" he said, when his plate was clean. "Can we have these at home, Mom?"

When the waiter brought out an enormous honey and banana cake, Mom lit the candles on top. Everyone sang Happy Birthday to Max. The noise was deafening!

Max blew out the candles with one big breath! "Aunt Zelda's missed a great party," said Dad, as he took a photograph. "I'm not so sure about that," said Mom.

When it was time to leave, Mom wrote a thank you note to Aunt Zelda and tucked it into the bear's pocket. He gave them a friendly smile (well, they *still* hoped it was a friendly smile). Then they waved to the other guests and shouted goodbye.

"Hello, Cocky," said the cockatoo, as she returned Dad's hat.

Mom led the way down the path, back to the car. This time Max and Kelly weren't afraid of the shadows that stretched across the pathway.

All night long, Max and Kelly dreamed about the Zoo Room.
Kelly wished they could go there for her birthday too.
But in the morning there was some bad news.

"There'll be no more parties at the Zoo Room," said Mom. "Aunt Zelda's in a bit of trouble."

Max and Kelly were sad about the Zoo Room, but it wasn't all bad. Perhaps someone would find the tiger . . .

. . . and they could visit the bear, the monkeys and all the others at the zoo whenever they wanted.

Maybe they would even find Aunt Zelda and get her recipe for barbecued insects.

After all,
Max would *never* forget his special
birthday dinner. Ever!